YOU CAN Do it MAX!!
I CAN Do it!!

This book is dedicated to you, the reader.
I hope today you feel included and loved.
You are amazing.

In memory of Grandma Debbie Heath Scholl and
Grandpa Michael Scholl.

A special thank-you to all of Max's therapists.

www.mascotbooks.com

Hi, Max

For more information, please contact:
Mascot Books, an imprint of Amplify Publishing Group
620 Herndon Parkway #320
Herndon, VA 20170
info@mascotbooks.com

Library of Congress Control Number: 2021925892

CPSIA Code: PRT0322A
ISBN-13: 978-1-63755-036-6

Printed in the United States

Hi, Max

Malena Heath Lindberg

Illustrated by Alejandro Echavez

Hi, everyone! My name is Malena.

I'm nine years old. I live with my parents; my four-year-old twin brothers, Max and Major; a dog; and a cat.

When my brother Max was seven months old, he was diagnosed with cerebral palsy (CP). His doctor, Dr. Gaebler-Spira at Shirley Ryan AbilityLab, told us CP affects each person differently.

She wanted Max to do a lot of physical, occupational, and speech therapy, and she told Max she believed in him. I want to be like her when I grow up to help other families like ours.

Sometimes my brother needs the support of a hospital, like Central DuPage. In the emergency room (ER), Nurse Taylor is usually the first to greet him with, “Hi, Max!” Even when he’s not feeling well, the greeting usually brings him a smile. When Max is admitted, it is Dr. Z who welcomes him with, “Hi, buddy.” After seeing all the times doctors and nurses have helped his twin brother, Major says he wants to work in the ER.

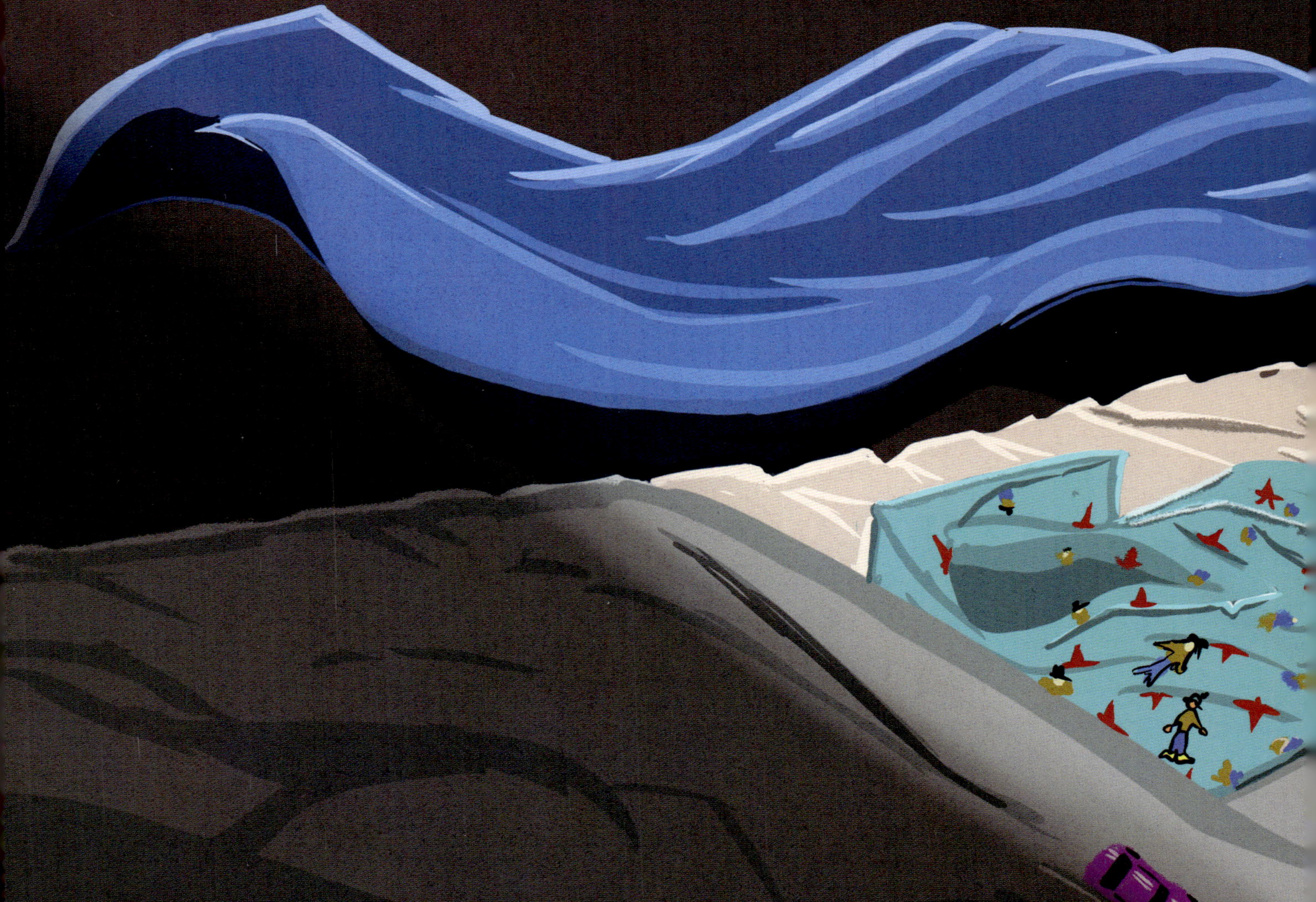

There are times, though, when Max gets frustrated, upset, and scared—just like all of us do. So as a family, we keep our eyes on his needs and watch for his wants because helping and caring for him is one way we let Max know how much we love him.

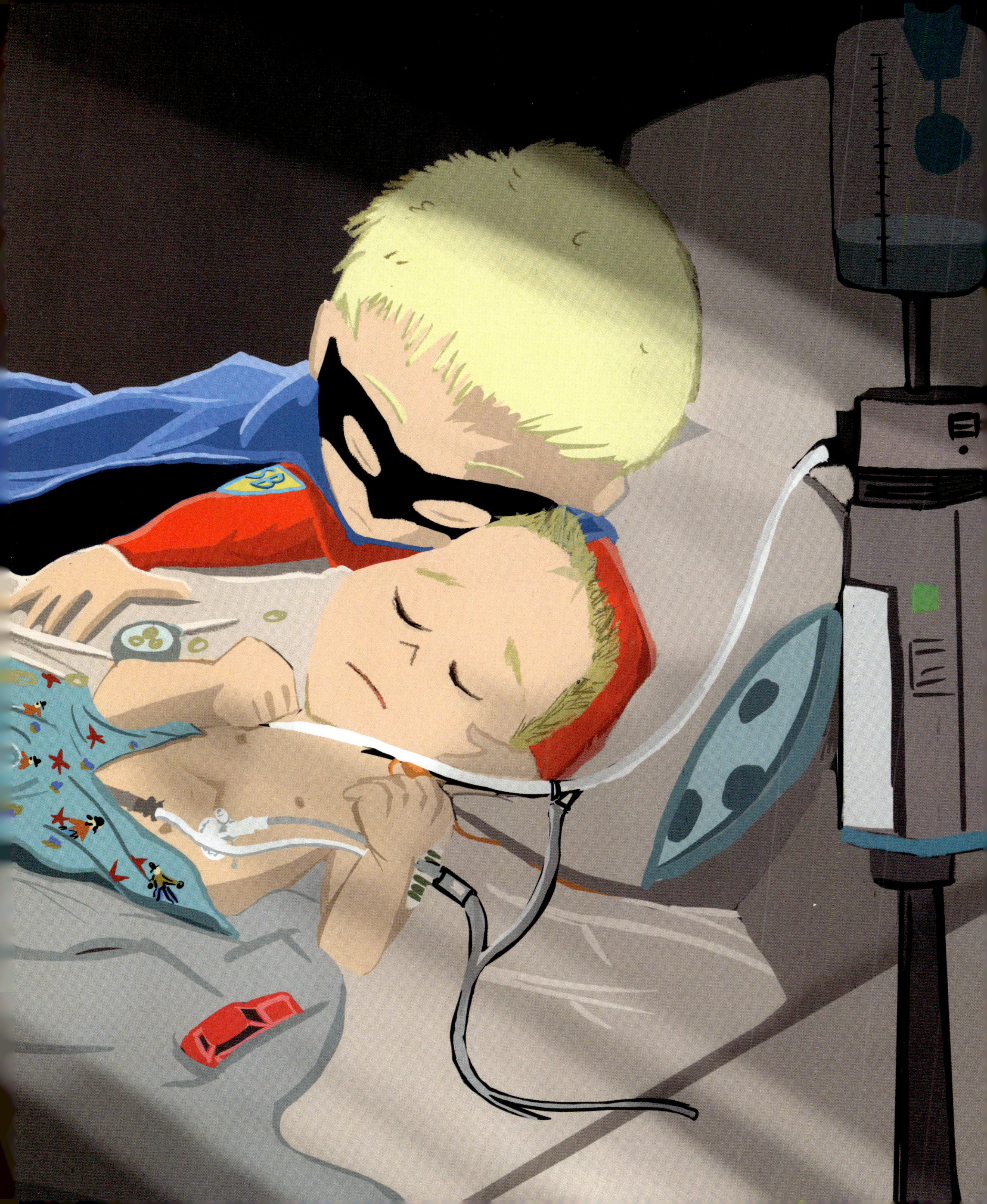
SB

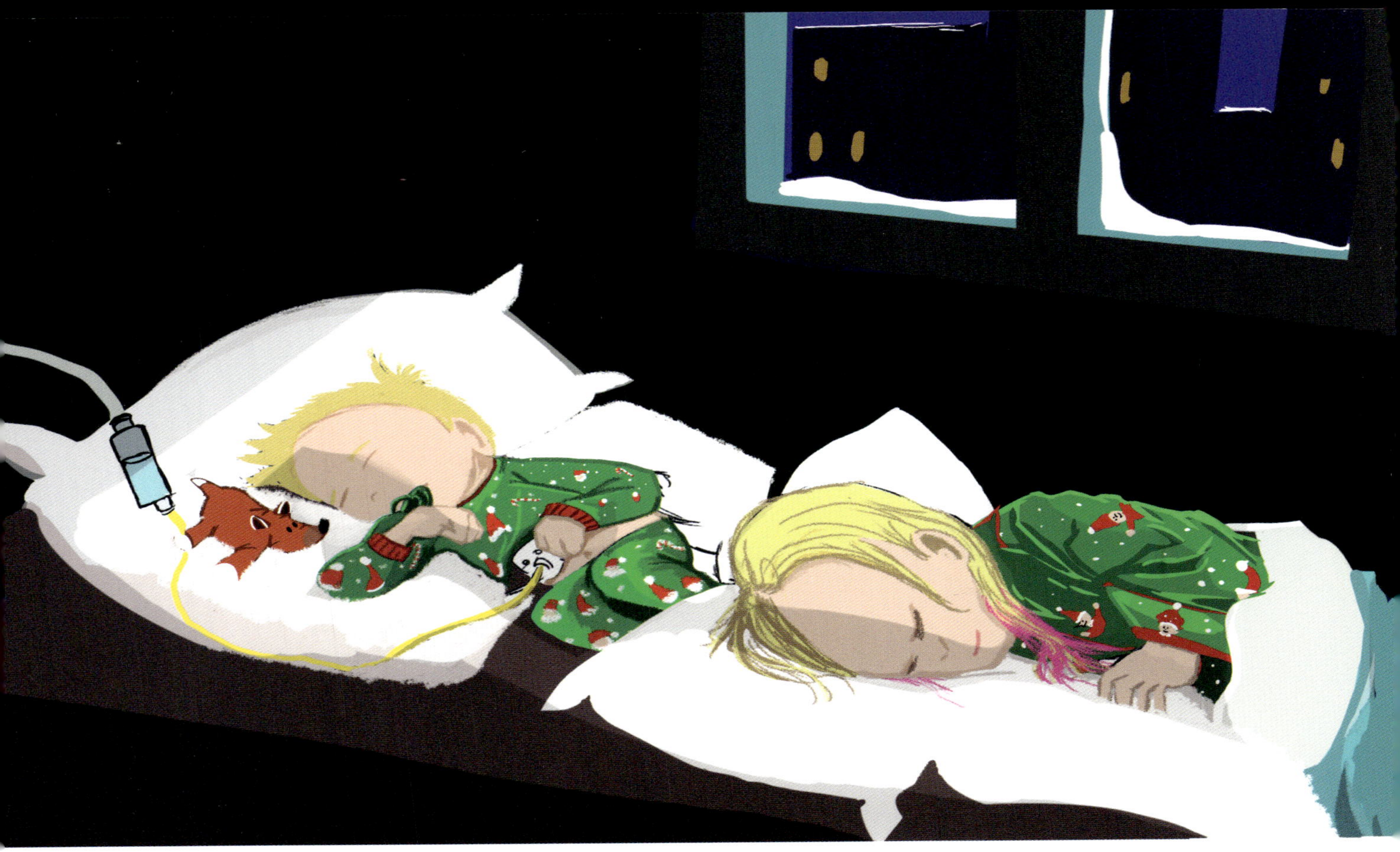

Max is fed through a feeding tube in his belly. He uses a manual and a power wheelchair. He also uses a gait trainer, which provides him standing and walking support.

Happy Birthday
Hi MAX

Happy Birthday

One way Max communicates is by shaking his head for no and raising his right arm for yes. We ask him yes and no questions a lot.

He also is working on using a communication device that he controls with his eyes. How cool is that? But Max's smile is my favorite communication. From sunup to sundown, his smile guides us and shows us his love.

My brother Max is disabled. It's a part of who he is; it's a part of human diversity. We learn from Max how to advocate with him.

Major and I get very excited when we see a ramp outside a house or building or when we see another wheelchair accessible van on the road, and we all cheer when a playground is accessible. I am so proud of Max, and I want to do so many things with him.

Life is way more fun when everyone is included.

What I love most about Max is that he is sweet, easygoing, laughs at silly stuff, and loves to be near me. When we are together at home, we have shaving cream fights in his stander, have watercolor painting sessions, play hide and seek, freeze dance, play board games, and watch WWE. Max wants to be a WWE wrestler! But his favorite part of the day is going to John Schroder Early Childhood Center with Major.

What I fear most is that my brother will be bullied, left out, or unwelcome. Sometimes I see kids avoid him, but I hope more and more kids choose to play with him. I'm also sad that people stare at him. Even at everyday places—at the grocery store, park, and doctor's office—the stares can make him feel like he doesn't belong.

We feel that negative energy, and it hurts. He does belong, so instead of staring at him, say, "Hi, Max." "Hi" feels welcoming and safe. It feels good, just like when someone says hi to you.

I know life can be difficult, but I promise it's beautiful too. "Hi" is one way to make this possible. Hi, Max!

HOLA MAX!
Hi Max!
Hi Max!!
Hi Max

Hi, Max
SANTA
Hi, Max!

Lucky Shot
CONDUCTOR
1017
You Rock MAX!!
HI MAX!
Hi MAX!
Hi, Max!
Hi Max!!

Hi MAX!!
HI MAX

Hi, Max!
I Traveling
Hi Max!!

Hi, Max!
Hi Max

Hi, Max!

Hi Max!!
Paris
Hi, Max!
MAX

Hi, Max!

Hi, Max!

About the Author

Malena has been on a mission to encourage "Hi, Max" in everyday situations since she was six years old. She spoke at summer camps, libraries, her first-grade classroom, and she made a video that featured people all around the world saying hi to her brother Max. Malena loves being a big sister and is looking forward to a life of adventure with her brothers.

himax.com

@maxtheeffect HiMax